Walt Disney's Pinocchio

Illustrated by the Disney Storybook Artists
Adapted by Kate Hannigan

Published by
Louis Weber, C.E.O.
Publications International, Ltd.
7373 North Cicero Avenue
Lincolnwood, Illinois 60712

Ground Floor, 59 Gloucester Place
London W1U 8JJ

Customer Service: 1-800-595-8484 or customer_service@pilbooks.com

www.pilbooks.com

p i kids is a registered trademark of Publications International, Ltd.

Manufactured in China.

ISBN-10: 0-7853-9542-3
ISBN-13: 978-0-7853-9542-3

Some people don't believe that wishes can come true. Jiminy Cricket felt that way. That is, until something happened that made him change his mind.

It all began in a quiet little town, deep in a valley. The whole village was asleep except for an old woodcarver named Geppetto. The light from Geppetto's fireplace seemed inviting, Jiminy thought, and so he went inside.

The woodcarver's workshop was filled with the most amazing toys and music boxes. Suddenly a door opened, and Geppetto came into the room with his cat, Figaro. He put some finishing touches on a puppet. "Now I have just the right name for you," Geppetto said. "Pinocchio!"

The woodcarver danced with the puppet, and Figaro the cat and Cleo the fish joined them. Soon it was bedtime, and Geppetto climbed into bed. He looked over at the wooden boy and thought Pinocchio almost seemed alive. Wouldn't it be nice if he were a real boy, Geppetto thought.

Geppetto was tired and ready to sleep. As he gazed out the open window, he saw the wishing star shining in the night sky. He made a wish:

Star light, star bright, first star I see tonight
I wish I may, I wish I might
Have the wish I make tonight.

Geppetto asked Figaro if he could guess what he'd wished for. Geppetto told the cat that he hoped Pinocchio might become a real boy. The old woodcarver smiled as he drifted off to sleep.

Jiminy Cricket was curled up nearby in a cuckoo clock. Geppetto's wish was sweet but not at all practical, Jiminy said to himself.

Suddenly a bright light filled the room. It was the Blue Fairy! She said Geppetto deserved to have his wish come true because he had made others so happy. The fairy gently tapped the wooden puppet with her magic wand, and he came to life. Pinocchio could walk and talk!

Pinocchio asked the Blue Fairy if he were a real boy. The fairy said she'd given Pinocchio life because Geppetto had asked for it, but it was up to Pinocchio to become real. "Prove yourself brave, truthful, and unselfish, and someday you will be a real boy," the Blue Fairy said.

The fairy told Pinocchio he would have to learn to choose between right and wrong. Pinocchio wasn't sure how he was supposed to know the difference, but the fairy said his conscience would tell him. "What is a conscience?" Pinocchio asked.

Jiminy Cricket tried to explain it, but it was difficult. The Blue Fairy told Jiminy he could be Pinocchio's conscience — the keeper of the knowledge of right and wrong, a guide along the straight and narrow path. She waved her wand and turned Jiminy's rags into a nice suit.

"Now Pinocchio," the Blue Fairy said, "be a good boy, and always let your conscience be your guide." And then she disappeared into the night.

Jiminy Cricket wanted to get right down to business, so he began to lecture Pinocchio on following his conscience. He told his friend to give a little whistle whenever he needed Jiminy. Before long, the two friends woke up Geppetto with their whistling and singing.

The woodcarver asked who was there, and Pinocchio answered him. "Oh, all right," said Geppetto, rolling over to go back to sleep. Suddenly he jumped out of bed. Who could it possibly be, he wondered. When he walked into the woodshop, there was Pinocchio standing before him. Geppetto thought it must be a dream—a wonderful dream!

Pinocchio could talk, and he told Geppetto all about the Blue Fairy and his conscience. He said that someday he was going to be a real boy. Geppetto was so happy that his wish had been granted. Geppetto danced around his woodshop again. There was much to celebrate.

Once they settled down for the night, Geppetto told Pinocchio to have a good sleep. Tomorrow, Pinocchio would be going to school.

When morning came, the children of the town hurried by on their way to school. Geppetto told Pinocchio they were his schoolmates — real boys and girls. Pinocchio couldn't wait to go to school and meet them. Off he skipped with his books and a shiny red apple.

But along the way, Pinocchio met some troublemakers. A sly fox called Foulfellow and a cat called Gideon convinced Pinocchio that the theater was the place for him. They told him he should become an actor. Pinocchio thought it sounded fun, so he walked down the road with the two scoundrels.

Jiminy Cricket leapt out of bed and ran after Pinocchio. It was his first day on the job, and he was late! Jiminy tried to catch up with Pinocchio, shouting and calling after him. Finally he whistled. "That's my conscience," Pinocchio told Foulfellow. But as hard as Jiminy Cricket tried, he could not keep Pinocchio from becoming an actor.

Foulfellow took Pinocchio to meet the evil puppet master Stromboli. Stromboli took one look at Pinocchio and rubbed his hands together. He knew he would make a fortune off this puppet without strings.

That night Stromboli put on a special performance, and the audience loved Pinocchio. They cheered and threw coins onto the stage. Stromboli was rich. As he counted his money after the show, he told Pinocchio he could never leave. "You belong to me now," Stromboli said.

Pinocchio was sad. He wanted to see his father. He
began to whistle as loud as he could. Finally Jiminy
Cricket hopped by his side. Jiminy said it would take a
miracle to free Pinocchio.

Suddenly a bright light shone before them, and the Blue
Fairy appeared. She asked Pinocchio why he didn't go to
school. Pinocchio told her a lie, and his nose began to
grow. With each lie he told, his nose grew longer and
longer until it was long enough for birds to nest on it!

The Blue Fairy told Pinocchio that a lie keeps growing until it's as plain as the nose on your face. Pinocchio was ashamed, and he promised not to tell another lie. The fairy rescued Pinocchio, but she said it was the last time.

Pinocchio and Jiminy Cricket ran as fast as they could back to Geppetto. But before they got home, Pinocchio met up with Foulfellow again. This time, Foulfellow pretended to be a doctor. He told Pinocchio he needed a vacation to Pleasure Island, where boys could skip school and waste the day away. The last coach was leaving at midnight, he told Pinocchio. They were running late.

Pinocchio climbed aboard the noisy coach full of boys and rode it all the way to Pleasure Island. He made friends with a boy called Lampwick. "Being bad is a lot of fun," Pinocchio told him as they got into mischief.

Suddenly the boys sprouted donkey ears and tails, and Pinocchio's laugh sounded like the bray of a donkey!

Jiminy Cricket saw what was happening. All the boys were turning into donkeys. They had to get out of there right away. Jiminy grabbed Pinocchio, and they scrambled over a wall and dove right into the ocean. They swam all the way home.

When they reached Geppetto's woodshop, Pinocchio called to his father. But the house was empty. He had gone looking for Pinocchio. A letter fluttered down from the sky as if by magic and landed at Pinocchio's feet. "It says here that your father was swallowed by a whale!" read Jiminy Cricket. Geppetto was trapped in the whale's belly and living at the bottom of the sea.

Pinocchio rushed to find his father. Jiminy Cricket warned Pinocchio that it was too dangerous, but Pinocchio wanted to go anyway. Jiminy decided to join him. "I may be live bait down there, but I'm with you," Jiminy said. Pinocchio and Jiminy Cricket jumped into the water and sank to the ocean floor.

Inside the belly of the giant whale, Geppetto and Figaro were searching for fish to eat. Finally the whale swam after some tuna and scooped them up in his giant mouth. Monstro the Whale scooped up Pinocchio, too.

Geppetto was surprised to see Pinocchio after so long. He hugged his boy, and Figaro and Cleo jumped for joy. Pinocchio said he could help Geppetto get out of the whale's belly. "We'll make him sneeze," Pinocchio said, setting fire to some wood and creating a thick blanket of smoke.

Monstro let out a mighty sneeze and shot Pinocchio, Geppetto, Figaro, and Cleo right out! They swam for safety, but the whale tried to swallow them back up. Pinocchio and Geppetto paddled as fast as they could on a makeshift raft as Monstro chased them.

Geppetto grew tired and told Pinocchio to save himself. Pinocchio couldn't leave his father. It took all his strength, but Pinocchio was able to pull Geppetto onto the shore. Once his father was safe, Pinocchio collapsed.

Geppetto carried Pinocchio home and laid him on the bed. The Blue Fairy appeared and whispered to Pinocchio. "Prove yourself brave, truthful, and unselfish, and someday you will be a real boy," she said. And with the touch of her magic wand, Pinocchio sat up.

Geppetto wiped away his tears. Pinocchio was alive! He was a real boy!

The Blue Fairy gave Jiminy Cricket a gold medal for being Pinocchio's conscience, and Jiminy wears it every day. It helps remind him that wishes really can come true.